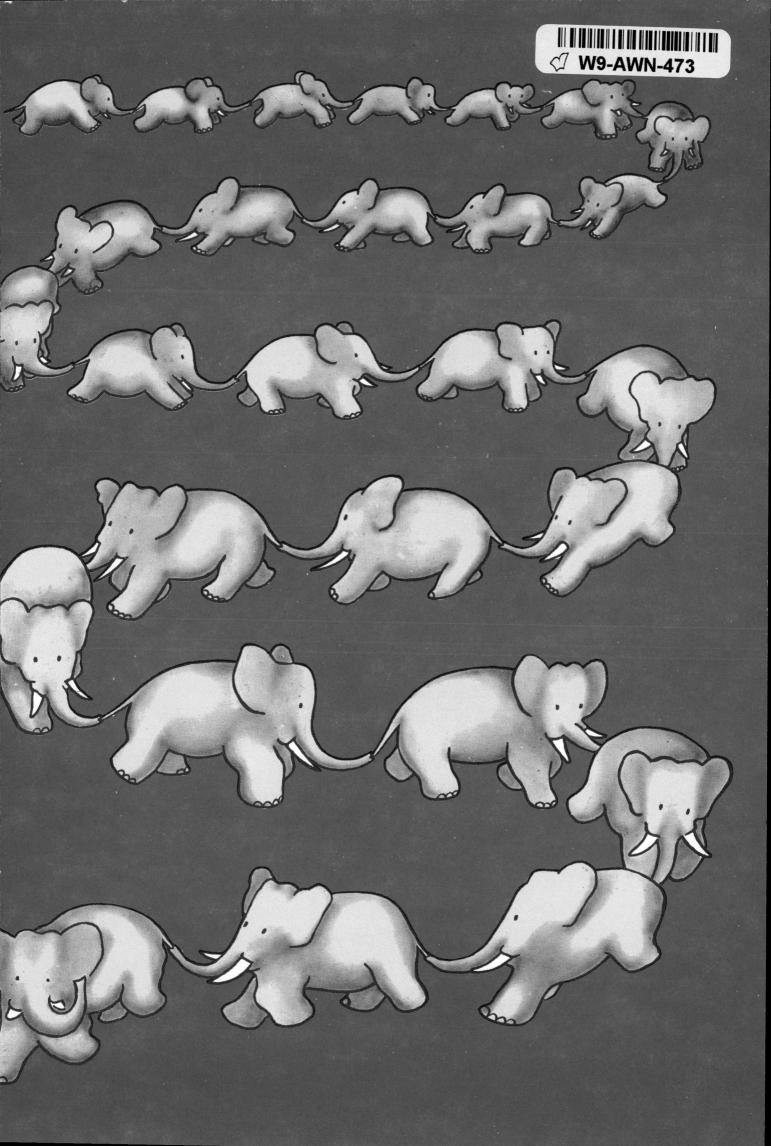

Other Babar Books

Beginner Book

Pop-Up Books

LAURENT DE BRUNHOFF

BABAR'S
BIRTHDAY SURPRISE

Random House, Inc., New York

In the country of the elephants, Podular, the sculptor, is finishing a pretty little statue of his friend King Babar. Zéphir, the monkey, watches without making a sound.

But suddenly — *tap! tap! tap!* — someone knocks on the door. Queen Celeste enters with the Old Lady and Cousin Arthur.

The little statue is finished, and Podular goes to the door with his visitors. Celeste lets Babar walk on ahead with the Old Lady. Then she speaks to the sculptor in a low voice.

"My dear Podular," she says, "I would like to give Babar a surprise for his birthday. Here is my idea. Will

you carve a giant statue of King Babar right in the side of the mountain?"

"Bravo! Bravo!" cry Arthur and Zéphir.

Podular is very enthusiastic too.

"But take care," adds Celeste. "Babar must suspect nothing!"

Aided by Zéphir, Podular loads his truck. Without losing a minute, they leave for the mountain.

Finally they find a place where the stone seems well suited for carving. They cut down some trees and raise a scaffolding against the mountain.

Suddenly two marabous perch beside them.

"What are you doing here?" they cry. "We are planning to build our nest on this mountain!"

But when they learn that Podular is going to carve a large statue of Babar in the rock, they click their beaks joyously and declare that they are ready to help.

A cry from Zéphir interrupts them. "Babar!" he shouts. "Babar is coming this way on his bicycle!"

Podular had forgotten that Babar often took this road to go fishing. Fortunately it leads behind the mountain so Babar sees nothing.

But Podular is upset all the same. He calls the two marabous.

"Would you be good enough to stand guard?" he asks.

"Then I won't have to worry."

Césarine, the giraffe, is very excited by the adventure. She stands watch with the marabous, too.

Podular has carved Babar's crown. Now he is working on one of the eyes with his pneumatic drill, while Zéphir swings on the rope. Suddenly a horn toots.

"Look out!" cries the giraffe. "It's Babar!"

However, the sculptor does not seem to be worried.

"It's all right, Césarine," he says calmly.

"Take a good look."

It is not Babar who is coming at all. Podular and the little monkey have recognized the horn of Arthur's red car. They climb down to welcome him.

"We are getting along well, aren't we?" Zéphir calls to him. "You know, Babar just went by."

Arthur doesn't believe his ears.

"What? And he saw the statue?"

But Podular reassures him. "Not at all, Arthur," he says. "The secret is well kept. Your friend Zéphir is nothing but a tease. Now enjoy yourselves, but don't bother me."

The head of the statue is completely finished. Podular is working hard on Babar's necktie. "At least the most difficult part is done," he thinks.

Suddenly the marabous begin to cry out again.

"Someone is coming by bicycle!"

Arthur holds his breath...

"All is lost," sighs Podular.

But no. It is three bicycles—
not one—that are stopping
at the foot of the mountain.
Babar's children have come
to see the statue.

"Hi, Alexander! Pom!
Flora!" Podular cries to them.
"It is nice of you to come
see us."

"Oh! How handsome Papa is
as a mountain!" says Alexander.

Finally Podular is nearly finished with his work. He
has climbed down to carve the feet.

"It is time for a picnic!" cry the children.

Back in Celesteville everyone is very busy. Babar's birthday is to be a wonderful celebration. Poutifour, the gardener, waters his flowers.

"I can be proud of my flower beds," he declares.

In the palace kitchens, the Old Lady and Celeste come to see the cooks. No doubt about it—the cakes will be delicious.

Babar and Celeste take a walk together.

Celeste is nervous because Babar is so deep in thought. "Does he suspect something?" she wonders.

But Babar tells her that he is upset about losing his pipe the other day when he went fishing. Celeste promises herself that she will give him a beautiful new pipe.

Meanwhile Cornelius rehearses for the concert to be given on the great day.

On the very top of the mountain, behind the head of the
statue, Podular and his friends are enjoying their picnic.
They can see the city, the palace, and the river off in the
distance. But who is coming up the road by bicycle?

It is Babar! This time it is really he. Catastrophe! Will the secret be discovered at the last moment?...

Flora and Alexander, who are playing below, hide in the underbrush.

"I am looking for my pipe," Babar says to the giraffe. "I wonder if it fell around here? The other day I felt something slip from my pocket, but I didn't pay any attention."

With a flap of their wings, the marabous approach.

"A pipe will be hard to find in such a big place," says one.

"I was just playing with it," says the other. "Now where did I leave it?"

At that very moment, Flora steps on the pipe.

Hearing the noise, Babar turns around. "What was that?" he asks.

"I am afraid I just stepped on your pipe," one of the maribous answers quickly.

Immediately the two birds bring Babar the pieces of his pipe, while Flora and Alexander try to make themselves small behind the bushes.

"Ah, thank you, gentlemen," exclaims Babar. "I really love this pipe. I will glue it together again."

"Saved! Babar did not see the statue!" cry the children. In their joy, they jump wildly about on the scaffolding.

"Stop that, you little mischiefs!" scolds Podular. Too late — one board slides, and then the whole scaffolding collapses! What a fall! They are all a little stunned.

"Arthur has hurt his trunk," says the sculptor. "We must go fetch Doctor Capoulosse."

Zéphir jumps into the red car and drives off. In no time at all, he returns with the doctor.

Capoulosse examines Arthur. "It is not serious," he says. He puts some Mercurochrome on the wound. Then he gently rolls a long bandage all around the trunk.

"I think it would be a good idea to take him back to Celesteville for a little rest," he adds.

"Oh! Doctor, you won't say anything to Babar, will you?" asks Arthur nervously.

"No, no, little one, don't worry. I will not say a word."

Left alone with Zéphir, Podular tidies up all his tools and his ladders. Then he calls the marabous.

"Dear friends," he says. "Tomorrow is Babar's birthday. Will you ask the birds to hide the statue until the signal is given? Cornelius will lead a gay fanfare."

The following day
a crowd of elephants
head toward the mountain.
Babar is very happy.
"How nice of you, Celeste,
to organize this celebration!
I love to lunch on the grass."
Celeste smiles. She is thinking
that soon Babar will be even
happier. And the Old Lady has
a mysterious little smile on
her face, too.

As they draw near, Babar sees millions of birds covering the mountainside. He finds the spectacle very beautiful. Astonished, he asks, "Are they part of the festival, too?"

"Of course," Celeste answers. "They came just for your birthday. Everybody wanted to come. For, as you will see, there is a surprise..."

"Oh, yes, a surprise," repeats Cornelius as he trots away.

Cornelius assembles the musicians of the Royal Guard. One! Two! Three! The trumpets sound the fanfare. At this signal all the birds covering the mountain fly up at the same time. The air is filled with the loud fluttering of wings.

Babar is stupefied. "Why, it's me!…Extraordinary!" he says, hugging Celeste. "What a splendid statue. Podular, my friend, I congratulate you. Dear Celeste, I am very moved. What an enormous surprise!"

After lunch the cooks from the palace bring an enormous cake.

"Happy birthday!" the children shout.

Then Cornelius says, "Babar, it is up to you to cut the cake."

"Oh, yes, quickly," adds Arthur, sounding funny because of the bandage on his trunk.

Everyone cries, "Happy birthday! Happy birthday!"

Except for the weary Podular, who is fast asleep.

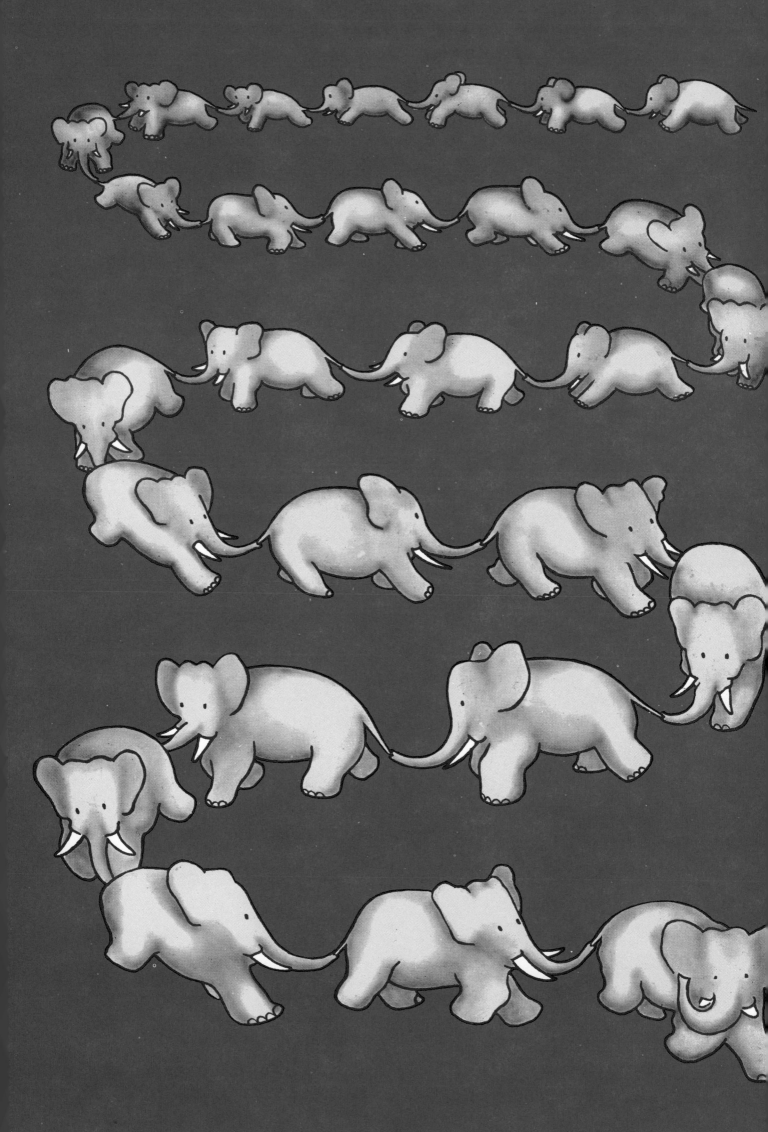